TO.

BUSY BABY

6/97

LC 3-12-04

By Naomi McMillan

Illustrated by Fred Willingham

Infant or toddler—age one, two, or three—
my child will always be "Baby" to me!

—*Anon.*

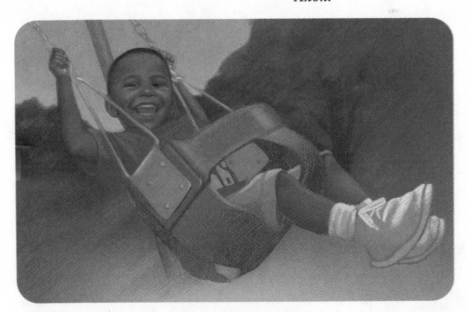

This Golden Book® was published in cooperation with Essence Communications, Inc.

A Golden Book • New York
Golden Books Publishing Company, Inc., Racine, Wisconsin 53404

It's early in the morning
and Baby is awake,
begging her big sister
to please play patty-cake.

Baby laughs and wiggles
and wrinkles up his nose,
as Mommy gently puts him
into bright play clothes.

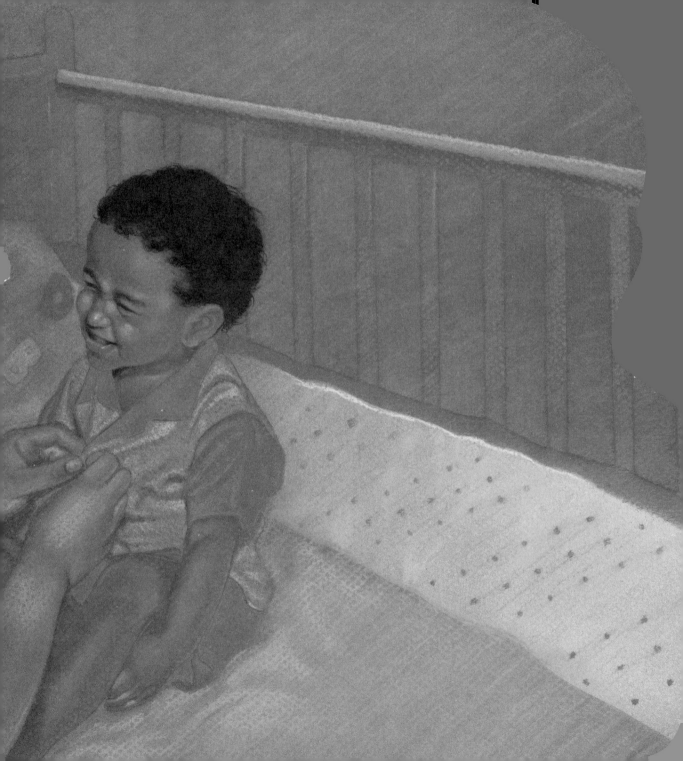

Baby's in the stroller,
exploring all the streets.
Baby waves and says hello
to everyone she meets.

Baby goes with Daddy
to a park nearby.
Daddy puts him in a swing
and pushes him up high!

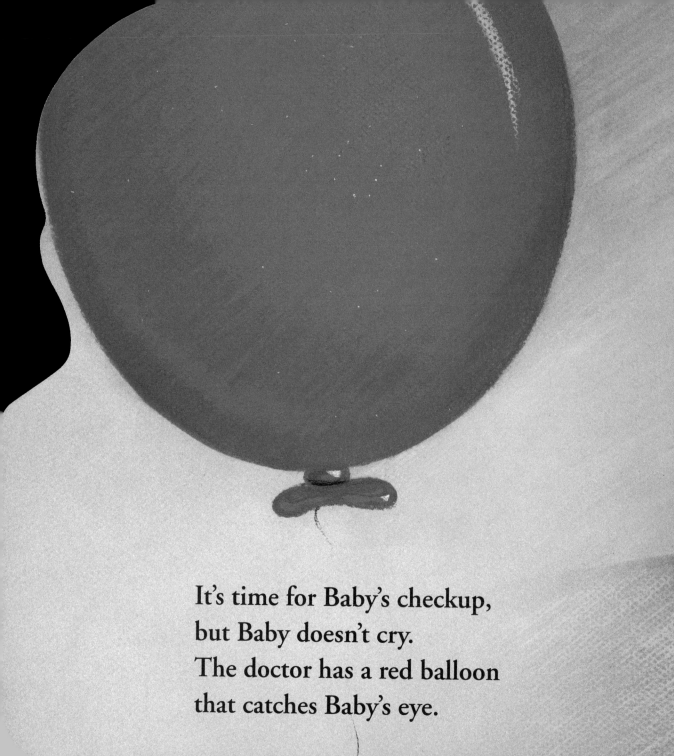

It's time for Baby's checkup,
but Baby doesn't cry.
The doctor has a red balloon
that catches Baby's eye.

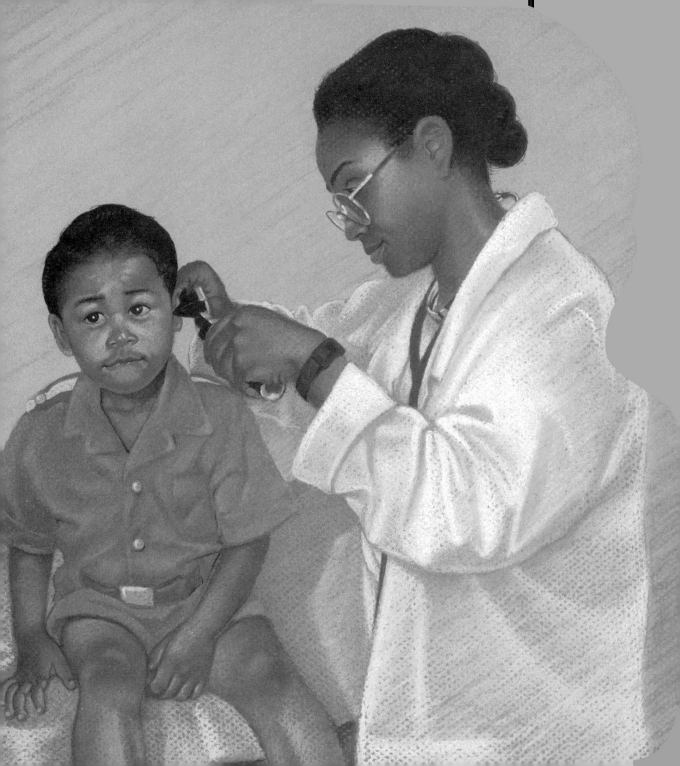

Little Baby's growing up.
She eats with her own spoon.
But where does Daddy find her food?
All around the room!

Baby loves her brand-new doll.
She combs and braids her hair.
When Baby's sister wants to play,
Baby says, "We share."

Baby loves to color
in his special book.
"What's that, sweetheart?" Grandma asks.
So Baby lets her look.

Daddy plays the piano
with Baby on his knee.
Baby wants to play along
and hits the highest key!

The tub is full of bubbles
that tickle Baby's skin,
Baby kicks and splashes,
making Mommy grin.

Storytime is special.
Baby learns a rhyme
of kings and queens in Africa
born in a far-off time.

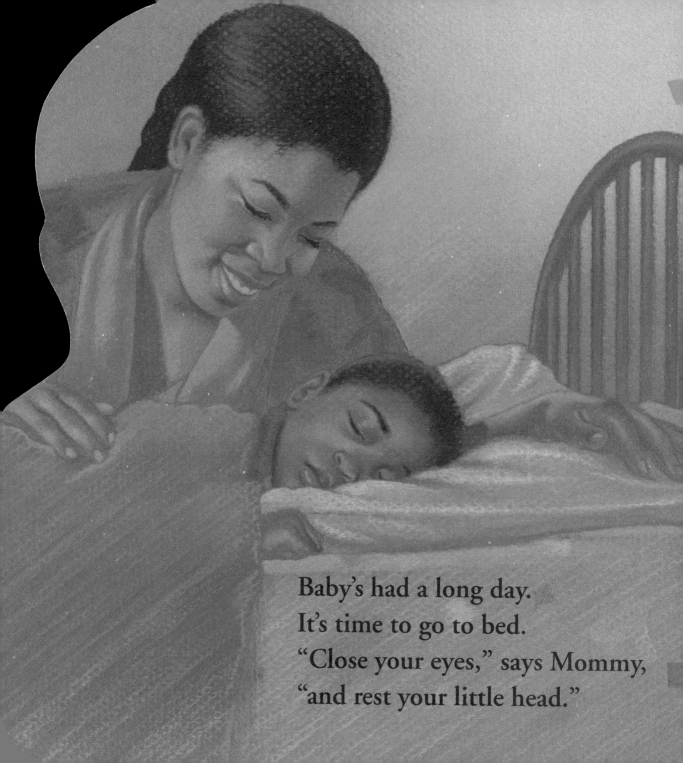

Baby's had a long day.
It's time to go to bed.
"Close your eyes," says Mommy,
"and rest your little head."